# Michael Tracey

## Freckles & Dara

Bumblebee
Books

BUMBLEBEE PAPERBACK EDITION



ISBN: 978-1-83934-865-5

*Bumblebee Books is an imprint of*
*Olympia Publishers.*

First Published in 2023

Bumblebee Books
Tallis House
2 Tallis Street
London
EC4Y 0AB

Printed in Great Britain
www.olympiapublishers.com

# Dedication

Dedicated to my niece, Malia Tracey

It was springtime and Farmer Jim was excited. The days were getting longer. The birds began to sing. The young rabbits played in the fields. The blanket of winter was giving way to new beginnings and new growth. Most of all, Farmer Jim looked forward to new life on his small sheep farm, sheltered by the protecting Killdoon Hills. On Monday morning, he stood by the sheep gate with his arms leaning over the top rail. His gray tweed peaked cap shielded his eyes from the morning sun as he gazed across the field, surveying his prized flock of sheep looking for any new arrivals. It was then that he heard a faint cry in the distance. He got excited. This was the moment he was waiting for. Opening the gate, he followed the faint bleating to discover a mother and her newborn daughter. That is where my story began.

Seeing that I was the first born, Farmer Jim looked at me and then my mother. Without hesitation, he called me 'Freckles.' I can understand why he gave me that name. You see, my mother's face was beautiful with freckles and I was happy to have inherited freckles too. And, above all, I really enjoyed the sound of the name. It had a joyful and happy feeling about it. Allow me to go back to the beginning, even before I was born. Before I was born, I lived in a very dark but comfortable place. I often wondered, was there life outside that place and, if there was, was it different or was it dark too? If it was dark outside, I didn't want to go outside, into more darkness. Then, one morning, it happened. My mother pushed and pushed until she pushed me out. And there I was, covered in a sort of blanket that I could barely see through. Then I felt my mother's warm tongue lick me all over. It felt warm and, somehow, I felt loved by my mother. Then I heard a voice, her voice, for the first time. She was actually talking to me and I could understand. She lay down beside me and offered me a gift that warmed my whole body.

Sometime later, I was able to stand up, even though I was a bit wobbly in the beginning. I learned to walk and even discovered I could jump and run around. This was so exciting. I was happy to be born. After all, this new world seemed different, not dark, like where I lived before. As I danced around, my legs got stronger. I jumped and jumped to show how happy I was. I would run away from my mother, not too far, because I wanted to explore but I always came back to her when she called me. I followed her around the field. She made sure I was safe and called out to me often to make sure I was protected.

A few days went by and I got stronger and stronger, thanks to my mother's milk. It was then that I discovered that I was no longer alone. One morning, I woke up to find another mother had a baby lamb during the night. Farmer Jim had noticed the new arrival too. Because the new arrival was a little different than me, Farmer Jim called him 'Brownie.' I wasn't sure why Farmer Jim gave him that name. Maybe, it was because the little boy lamb's fleece was a kind of tan or light brown color. Anyway, I was happy that I wasn't alone any longer and, maybe, the two of us might become friends.

Days passed and I watched Brownie get stronger and stronger like me. Like me, he kept close to his mother because he knew she would always protect him. In the beginning, I wanted to go over and talk to him but my mother didn't want me to go too far away from her, and, maybe, Brownie's mother might not want me too close to him. So, I had to be patient.

A few days later, I got brave and danced my way over to Brownie.
He seemed to be glad to see me. How do you greet another lamb? I
thought. Do you reach out one of your front paws like dogs do? How
do you tell another lamb that you want to be friends? I wasn't sure
but I decided 'nose to nose' might be the best way. Brownie seemed
to agree. And so our long friendship began.

Our mothers began to trust us. They were happy that we had
become friends even though as time went on, other lambs
were born as well. Our mothers gave us the freedom to meet
and talk about anything we wanted.
We began to meet and go off to a corner and just talk. We
could talk about anything because we trusted each other.
Sometimes, other lambs would come by and see that we were
busy talking. They would leave us alone and disappear again.

I remember one of the first conversations we had. It was early morning and the sun peeked out its head over the horizon. After we rubbed noses as part of our usual greeting, Brownie said, "You know we are different?"

"What do you mean?" I asked him. "Is it because you are a boy and I am a girl?"

"Not really," said Brownie. "Sure, we are different that way."

"Well," I asked, "is it because your skin is brown and mine is white?"

"That's it," he suggested.

"So, because we are different colors, does that mean we cannot be friends?" I asked Brownie.

I saw that he was getting a bit worried that, maybe, because we were different colors, we couldn't be friends any more. I wanted to let Brownie know that what was inside us was what really mattered, not the clothes we wore.
Brownie nodded his head in agreement, and I told him, "Color is something you wear, not who you are." He reached out and rubbed my nose for a long time. Then, I knew, he felt reassured that we could still be friends even though we were different on the outside. We were just different colors. I was happy that we had that conversation; that, somehow, we could not only trust each other but that there would be no barriers between us in the future. That night, I slept close to my mother, knowing that I was loved by her and that I had a very special friend who I loved.

The next morning, I awoke to a new day. Then I saw it spread across the morning sky.
It must be going to rain, I thought to myself. My mother called me to her side and we walked to a
place by a stone wall where we could take shelter until the rain was over.
"Did you see that beautiful, colorful bow across the sky?" I asked Brownie as we met.
"You mean, that thing with all the colors in it?" he asked.
"Yes," I said, "and do you know what it is called?"
"No, what is it called?"
"A rainbow," I told him.
"It was very beautiful with all those colors in it," said Brownie.
"It was! And do you know what made it so beautiful?" I asked him.
"Tell me," he said.

"It takes the sun and the raindrops to make a rainbow," I explained. "Both seem opposites and different. The sun gives the color to the raindrops inside it. And it makes the rainbow."
"We are like the rainbow," I continued. "Inside, we are lambs. We belong to the sheep family. We are the raindrops. When the sun shines on us,
our coats show our different colors."
It was then that I heard my mother calling me. It was feeding time again. As I parted ways with Brownie, we rubbed noses again. This was to be our secret code of friendship.
After feeding, it was time to take a nap. I lay down and thought about my conversation with Brownie about rainbows. I wondered if he was doing the same.

Days passed. New lambs arrived. The field came alive with different sounds of mothers calling for their newborns and newborns calling for their mothers. Then I noticed something amazing. I noticed in the middle of all the bleating of the newborns and their mothers, each mother recognized the bleat of her child and each child recognized the call of their mother. This was something new to me. I had recognized the call of my mother and she had recognized my call, days earlier. I had taken that for granted until I noticed how different and unique each bleat was when the field was filled with all those different bleating sounds. I was amazed how, in all that noise, sheep and lambs recognized each other's unique bleat. The next time, I met with Brownie, I had to share my new discovery. He agreed. He had noticed the same thing. By now, Farmer Jim's field was alive with the sound of bleating lambs. Like a musical score, each note was different and had a different cadence. Still, in the middle of such noise and differences, we still had something special in common.

Then, one day, Farmer Jim arrived with some new sheep. They didn't have any lambs at that time. I began to wonder, Would the sheep and lambs already in the field accept them?
After all, we were all sheep, even though some had lambs. Farmer Jim stood by the gate and seemed to be wondering the same thing. Would the new arrivals be accepted? We both watched for a while. The new arrivals stayed together at a distance from the rest of the sheep in the field. Maybe, they were wondering if they would be seen as foreigners or intruders. The sheep in the field already just kept doing what they were doing – moving about, eating grass, and calling their children to come close to them. It seemed to them as if the new arrivals didn't exist.This stand-off seemed to go on for a long time and no one seemed to want to welcome the new sheep. It was then that I decided to do something.

I ran to Brownie and asked him to help me. Both of us wanted to welcome the strangers but would our mothers allow us to go off by ourselves to meet the strangers? After all, our mothers didn't know or had never met the strangers. Maybe, they thought we shouldn't be around strangers – that the strangers might be jealous of us or, worse still, harm us. After all, our mothers were much older and wiser than two young kid lambs. I wondered, Should we listen to our mothers or listen to our hearts?

I also wondered what the new sheep might be thinking about the rest of us already in Farmer Jim's field. Would we be accepting? Hostile? Ignore them? Because we were there in the field first, were they thinking that we didn't want them eating our grass or did we feel threatened by their presence among us?

That night, I could hardly sleep thinking about how both Brownie and I would sneak away and meet the new arrivals without our mothers knowing or approving of it. Our plan was to meet up early in the morning while everyone else was asleep and go to meet the new arrivals.

Next morning, we discovered there was a new arrival among the strangers – another baby lamb just like us. She was born during the night. We could see that she was dancing around already. She must have really enjoyed her first full breakfast from her mother. If we could make friends with the new lamb, I thought, then, maybe, we could become friends with her mother. As we approached, the mother noticed us. She recognized that we didn't belong to her. Immediately, she put her head down, ready to challenge us and protect her little daughter. We just wanted to ask her if her little daughter could come and play with us. That is all! But the mother's instinct told her we were strangers. How were we going to gain her trust? How were we going to let her know that we came in friendship?The mother wasn't interested in our story. She put her head down and began to aim her long, curly horns toward us. We had no horns to protect ourselves so we ran back to our mothers. We hoped our mothers would protect us if that new lamb's mother ever came to attack us.

That night, I lay beside my mother, feeling loved and protected. I felt the warmth of her body as I drew close to her breast. Looking up at the night sky, I could see just a piece of the moon trying to light up the sky. It was surrounded by hundreds of small stars. Each of them, in their own way, was trying to light the dark world below. Why was there only a piece of the moon giving light? Why was it not giving more light? Was it sad? Was it afraid of the dark clouds that stopped it from shining its light on the world below?Those puzzling questions ran through my mind as I tried to go to sleep that night. I just had to accept that I may never know the answers but that would not stop me from trying to become friends with my neighbors no matter who they were.

When I woke the next morning, I couldn't feel my mother near me. I began to panic. Then, I saw her a few paces away, eating grass. I knew she was getting breakfast ready for me. She called me and off I ran to enjoy my breakfast. My little tail bobbed up and down as I showed how excited I was to have a fresh, warm breakfast to begin my day.As I finished my breakfast, I couldn't help but think about the new lamb and her mother among the stranger sheep Farmer Jim had put in the field with the rest of the sheep.

I had to find Brownie and tell him about the night sky I had watched before going to sleep.
"How did you sleep last night?" I asked him.
"Great," he said. "I just stretched out beside my mother and fell asleep straight away. I must have been really tired from all the running and jumping I did yesterday."
"Well, I didn't go to sleep straight away," I began, "even though I was tired too. I just lay there looking up at the beautiful night sky.""What was so beautiful about it?" asked Brownie."Oh! There was the moon. But I could only see part of it. Some clouds hid most of it," I replied. "But there were other lights in the sky too – smaller lights than the moon but they, too, lighted up the night sky. They were the stars.""They must have been pretty," suggested Brownie. "I'm sorry I missed them, I must have been too tired."
"When I sat lying there watching the moon and all the stars, I thought about how each of them, big or small, helped to light up the night sky and make it pretty."
"So, what do you think they – the moon and the stars – are trying to tell us?" asked Brownie as he cocked his head toward me.

"I'm not sure," I said. "Maybe, they are trying to tell us that no matter who we are, we can all help light up our own worlds. Even us sheep, we are all different. Some of us are sheep and some are lambs. Some of us are boys and some are girls. Some of us are white like me; some are brown like you; and some are even black. But what we have in common is that we are all sheep and, just like the moon and the stars at night, we need to get along because we are all part of the same family."
"Wow! I never thought of it that way," said Brownie. "For a little lamb, you are very wise. Maybe some of that wisdom might rub off on me."I just had to laugh at Brownie's innocence. We decided to rub noses – our secret greeting code – indicating that, no matter what happened, we would still remain friends, good buddies.

It was almost lunchtime and I was feeling hungry so I decided to call my mother to see
if she was ready to feed me. When I heard her call, I wasn't sure where she was as I
couldn't see her. Finally, she came running to me to make sure I was okay and
to feed me.After lunch, my mother moved off picking away at the green grass.
At times, I noticed that she bent down her two front feet to get closer to
the grass. It was then that, because the day was so beautiful,
I decided to stretch out and take a nap.
Sometime later – I am not sure how long – I awoke. It was getting dark.
I must have slept a long time. It was then that I sensed some strange creature coming toward
me. I began to panic and cried out. My mother heard me and knew it was a cry for help so she
came running toward me. As soon as she saw the stranger, she began to put her head down and
charged at the stranger. As soon as the stranger saw her fighting spirit,
she turned and ran away into the nearby woods.
When the danger was over, I thanked my mother for protecting me. But who was this stranger
and what did she want? Did she want us to be friends? I had never seen
anyone like her before. All the animals I knew up to now were animals like
myself – lambs and sheep.

I asked my mother to explain so I would know and be more careful in the future. She said, "We sheep like to eat grass. Sometimes, Farmer Jim gives us other things to eat – things he buys at the store. All these make us strong and healthy so we can feed you and protect you."

As I listened, she continued, "That stranger you saw didn't come to be your friend. She came to take you away from me.""How do you know that? Why would she want to do that?" I asked."She also has a family. I'm not sure how many she has but, like me, she has to feed them. Farmer Jim hates animals like her, as do I, because she steals his hens and even his little lambs to feed her young ones."I was shocked at what my mother was telling me. Maybe, I had been too naive, too trusting. I was happy that I had a mother who protected me and kept me safe.I was shaking all over and so scared. Yet, I felt so lucky because my mother knew what was about to happen to me and made sure I was safe.

As I tried to recover from the frightening experience, all kinds of questions and fears raced through my mind. Was I stupid to trust everyone? What about Brownie? Maybe, he was out to hurt me too? I didn't want to believe that he might, but now I wasn't sure any more. And what about Farmer Jim? Could I trust him? I suppose the only one I could trust was my mother. After all, she was the one who saved me. Maybe, I should listen to her some more and not be so stubborn. I lay there thinking for a long time. At the same time, I made sure my mother didn't go too far away so I could run to her if I was in danger again.

It was then that I saw Brownie coming toward me. What should I do? Should I ignore him or tell him directly that I didn't know if I could trust him or anyone else, except my mother, any more? "You look different," Brownie muttered. "You look scared. Did something happen to you? You are shaking all over." "I just don't know any more," I told him. "I don't know who to believe; who to trust any more. I am just scared to trust anyone."

"What do you mean?" Brownie asked. "What happened? You can tell me. You can trust me. Remember, after all, we are the best of friends. So, tell me what happened that made you so scared." Finally, I got the courage to tell Brownie about my lucky escape from the stranger that almost took me away from my mother. As Brownie listened, I saw tears begin to roll down from his eyes and down his face. Somehow, I knew then that I could still trust him. I knew that we could tell anything and everything to each other without feeling rejected.

When I finished telling Brownie about my scary experience, we both stood there for a while – just doing nothing or saying anything. We just needed to be together. Finally, Brownie broke the silence. "It is time for us to show our friendship no matter what." Then, we both shared our secret reminder of our friendship – we rubbed noses. Brownie went back to his mother.
As he left, he shouted at me, "Be safe."

I was getting hungry so I called my mother. I was glad that she didn't panic and think something terrible was happening to me again. She sensed that I was hungry and stood there while I drank my supper. When I was finished, my mother knew it would be getting dark so she lay down and asked me to lay by her chest so I could be safe. As I lay there, many thoughts and questions began to flood my mind again. There were some things I knew for sure. I knew that my mother loved me and would protect me with her life; I also knew that I could trust Brownie – no matter what happened to either of us, we would be there to trust and support each other. But what about the others? I found out that there were some I couldn't trust: some who were ready to kill me, some who would try to bully me, and even some that I could never be friends with or who wouldn't want to be friends with me.

I knew I couldn't change any of that, but I also knew that I had been given a very special gift and I was going to try and use it. I was going to try and make my little world a better place for everyone. I started by being friends with Brownie. As I told Brownie before, we were different – boy and girl; freckled faced and tan faced; different colors on the outside but beautiful lambs on the inside. Color was what we wore, not who we were. Soon, I fell asleep, knowing that I was safe in the arms of my mother. Tomorrow would be another day – a day to visit again with Brownie, my best friend; and, maybe, tomorrow might give me an opportunity and challenge to practice my special gift some more.

The morning sun almost blinded me as it peeked over the horizon. It said, "Wake up! Today is filled with possibilities. Enjoy them." It was as if the sun was telling me: "Here is another beautiful day to do some good, to enjoy your life with your friend, and to try and make some more friends. You do not want to waste the opportunities to be more trusting, more caring, more generous, more accepting, and less judgmental." So I called Brownie and he came running. I felt that the two of us should go to the stranger sheep and her lamb that Farmer Jim had put in our field days earlier. Maybe, when the mother sheep would see the two of us together, she might allow her new born lamb to come and play with us. We gave the new mother the name, 'Stubborn.' We felt that the name was best for her because she was very slow in trusting us. In a way, she was right to be 'Stubborn' because she wanted to be sure that anyone she let her little one play with could be trusted.

"Hi!" I began. "Let us introduce ourselves to you so you will know who we are. I am Freckles." "And I am Brownie. We are best buddies." "Can your little baby lamb come and play with us?" I asked.
"No! She cannot," said Stubborn.
"Why can't she come?" I asked again.
"You are too big for her. She is just a few days old and you might hurt her," replied Stubborn. "We'll be nice to her. We promise," I assured her. "You might be nice to her, as you say, but I'm not sure about your friend," Stubborn said in reply. "I'm not sure I can trust him." "What do you mean?" I asked about my friend.

"Well, I might begin to like you. You have such an innocent looking face. But, your friend—he is different. He is not like the rest of us with his chocolate looking face and coat."
"So? What is wrong with that?" I asked.
"Well, I'm not sure I can trust him. That's all," suggested Stubborn. "Do you not trust him because he is different, because he is brown-faced and has a brown coat? I asked. "Maybe?" "So, are you saying that as long as someone is white – like me, like you, like your daughter – then it is okay? But if someone has a different face or fleece, we should be suspicious of them; that we shouldn't trust them?" "Maybe, I am not sure. But he is different, your friend." I could see that Brownie wanted to say something, so I let him.

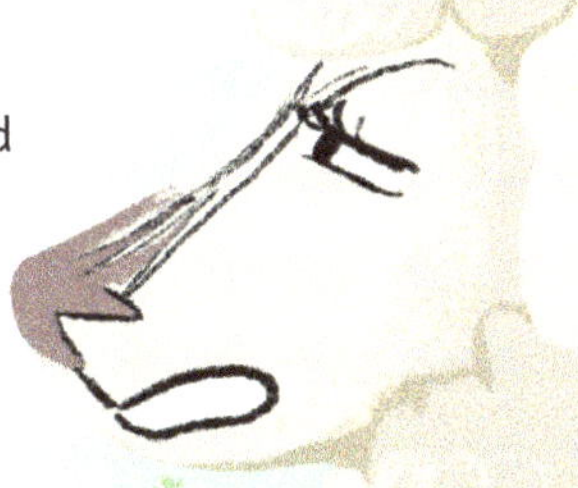

He said, "But aren't we all different? Some of us are boys and some are girls; some of us are older than the others. We all have different mothers and our mothers all have different lambs. Some have just one lamb. Some have twins. Some have triplets and maybe a few have quadruplets. But aren't we all part of one family, no matter how many brothers and sisters we have, no matter what the color of our skin is? We are all part of one very big sheep family and we should get along." I was surprised by what Brownie said. But it was true. It was what I believed and I wanted everyone to not be scared of each other because we were different. What made us different was what we shared in common, not our outward appearance. "Maybe what you say is true. Maybe you are right in saying that we need to get along; that we need to accept that we are all different. But it is hard for some of us to accept that and to trust each other," replied Stubborn. "I know it may be hard for you to think differently," I tried to explain to Stubborn. "I know you probably have been friends with the same kind of sheep for most of your life. Maybe you were more interested in surviving in this cruel kind of world. Maybe you were more interested in providing for your family all those years and making sure they were safe and well fed."

"Of course, I was," said Stubborn. "After all, that was my job."
"Of course, it was your job," Brownie explained. "But doing your job doesn't mean you can't be friends with other sheep. Of course, you can. Life is more than a job. It is also about relationships and relationships involve others, no matter what they wear." "But, you've got to be careful there," answered Stubborn. "You can't be friends with everyone. There are bad animals around. There are some who want to hurt you; some who want to bully you; and even some who want to kill you." When she mentioned 'kill you,' I thought about the near escape I had some days earlier; how my mother protected me from the stranger who wanted to grab me and kill me. I felt sad and scared, thinking back to that stranger who wanted to kill me. I looked at Stubborn and knew she was right. But all Brownie and I wanted was to invite her little daughter to come with us and play. Then she began again, "Let's do this. Let you and Brownie go off and play by yourselves. I need some time to think about all we have talked about. I want what is best for my daughter and I want to protect her as well. So, give me some time to think about it and we can talk some more later."

We nodded our heads in agreement. We could go off and play together and give Stubborn some time to think about things. At least, we knew she wasn't really stopping us from playing with her daughter. Maybe, when she had some time to think about things, she might be willing to let her daughter trust us and play with us.

Satisfied, we headed off to play together – both of us – and to enjoy the beautiful day.Two days later, Brownie and I headed back to see Stubborn. Was she willing to trust us and allow her daughter to come and play with us?

"Well," said Brownie, "have you thought about our conversation a few days ago?"
"I have.""And...?" Brownie paused, hoping to hear some good news.
"I thought a lot about our conversation. I was able to see that what both of you were saying really did make sense. I had wondered how come you were so wise and yet so young."
It was then that I said, "You see, when you are young, like us, everything is new. Everything is exciting. Everything is to be explored. We are very open, very trusting and that can be both good and bad. Hopefully, there is more good than bad in being more open and trusting." "I suppose you are right there," Stubborn commented. "Take us, old sheep, we are set in our ways. We just know a few basic things. We know how to be mothers; how to care for our children; and we know how to eat grass. That's it!" "And that's all good and needed," said Brownie. "Without you doing all the things you do for lambs like us, we wouldn't feel safe and secure. We will always appreciate all the things you do for us." "Well, thank you!" "So, are you ready to let your daughter come and play with us now?" I asked, hoping Stubborn would say 'yes.'

Aoife came to join us. We ran and danced around the field together. You may wonder why we decided to call our new friend, 'Aoife.' Well, 'Aoife' means 'beauty' and 'pleasure.' As we got to know her more and more, we could see how beautiful she was inside and out and that we enjoyed her company. Now, we were three special friends – Freckles, Brownie, and Aoife. We were a trinity of love.

Days, weeks, and months passed. We continued to make lots of friends and our family began to grow more and more. Together, we were changing the world, field by field. We didn't need our mothers as much any more. We grew more independent as well as grew in stature. By now, our mothers could see that we were enjoying life, breaking down barriers and having fun doing it.

Farmer Jim checked on us almost daily. He was happy that we were happy and enjoying ourselves. After all, it was springtime. Everything around us was beginning to wake up from a long winter sleep. Everything and everyone was beginning a new life.Life was good. Days grew longer and hopes for lasting friendships expanded. Both lambs and sheep began to see the beauty inside each other and to not judge each other by outward appearance.

My friendship with Brownie and Aoife grew and expanded. Color, age, and status didn't matter any more to anyone. We were all different on the outside but soulmates on the inside where it really mattered. Our world was filled with trust, love, acceptance, and sharing our gifts and uniqueness. We were rich in our diversity.

We lived in hope that all this could continue until one day something happened that changed everything. Farmer Jim arrived in the field with his black jeep. He towed a small trailer behind the jeep. Everyone got excited, sensing that Farmer Jim was about to put us all – lambs and mothers – into the trailer and take us to a new field where there would be lots of grass. All began to bleat with excitement and anticipation. There we could eat as much as we wanted, be lazy, and just grow old together. What a way to enjoy life, we thought. Farmer Jim opened the passenger door of his jeep and out sprang his dog – a black and white Border Collie. We knew Farmer Jim had trained his dog, Rover, to be a sheepdog since he was a little pup. We also knew that Rover's job was to gather us together and bring us to Farmer Jim's trailer without letting any of us
stray away.

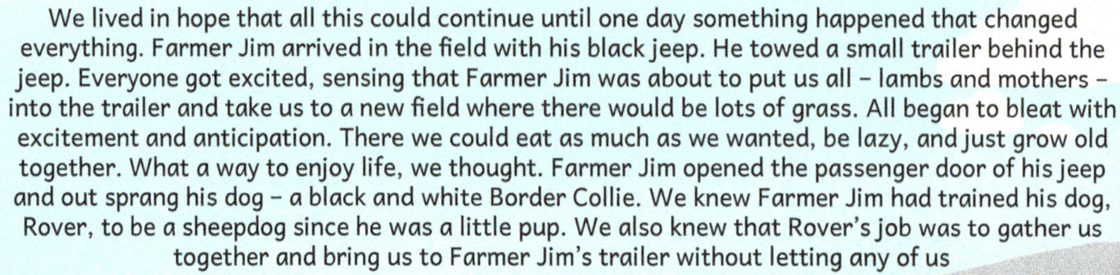

Farmer Jim let out a series of different whistles as commands for Rover to obey. I watched as Rover went to the end of the field to gather a few stray sheep and lambs. They didn't want to cooperate. Some even put down their heads and tried to bully Rover but he showed everyone he was the boss. Rover kept moving back and forth behind the sheep, keeping them moving toward Farmer Jim. Eventually, he ushered them into a tubular rectangular gathering place. We wondered what was about to happen. Mothers called out for their lambs and lambs did the same. In the midst of all the noise, I could hear my mother calling me. I called back to remind her that I was with my friends, Brownie and Aoife.

Farmer Jim stood in the middle of all of us and glanced around. Then he began to catch some of the lambs by their hind legs and usher them into the trailer as Rover stood guard, making sure that none of them escaped from the trailer.After a while, Farmer Jim stopped. He had separated some of the lambs from their grieving mothers as they called out to each other in vain.My mother called again for me. She was excited to hear my voice again, knowing I was not one of the lambs captured and put in Farmer Jim's trailer. It was then that I realized that Farmer Jim had separated the boy lambs from the girl lambs. He had put the boy lambs in his trailer.

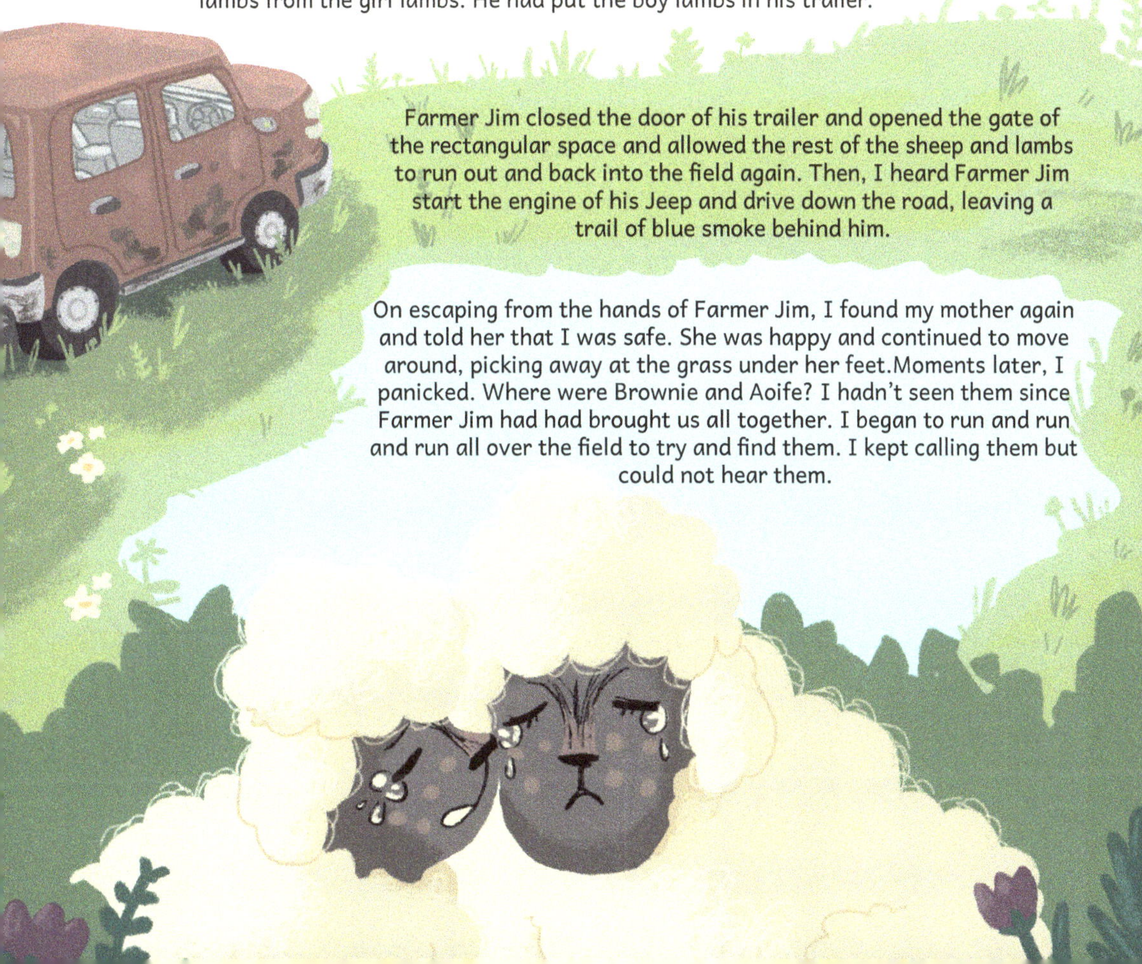

Farmer Jim closed the door of his trailer and opened the gate of the rectangular space and allowed the rest of the sheep and lambs to run out and back into the field again. Then, I heard Farmer Jim start the engine of his Jeep and drive down the road, leaving a trail of blue smoke behind him.

On escaping from the hands of Farmer Jim, I found my mother again and told her that I was safe. She was happy and continued to move around, picking away at the grass under her feet.Moments later, I panicked. Where were Brownie and Aoife? I hadn't seen them since Farmer Jim had had brought us all together. I began to run and run and run all over the field to try and find them. I kept calling them but could not hear them.

Exhausted from my search and about to give up, I lay down and started to cry. How could this happen to me? I went around doing good, making friends and all those friends are gone. I cannot find them. I cannot find Brownie and Aoife. Farmer Jim must have taken them off and I will never see them again.

The more I cried, the sadder I became. How could Farmer Jim take away my friends? He is a cruel and mean man. No one can trust him any more. What is the point in trying to make friends when they are taken away from you so suddenly? Maybe I should just give up. Maybe I should just lay down and die. I cried myself to sleep that night.

When I woke up the next morning, my eyes were still tired from crying and lack of sleep. I saw someone staring at me. My first instinct was to panic because I thought back to the strange animal who came to snatch me and how I was saved by my mother.

It was then that I heard a voice – a familiar voice. "Are you okay?" Aoife asked. "I was worried about you." "Oh! Is that you, Aoife?" I asked as I tried to shake myself awake. "Yes! Yes! It's me, Aoife, your friend. I lost you in the crowd yesterday when Farmer Jim came to take some of us away. I searched and searched all day for you yesterday after Farmer Jim left. I kept calling you but didn't hear from you so I crawled under a tree and just cried and cried because I had lost my best friend." "Oh, Aoife! I'm so happy to see you. I'm glad you didn't give up and stop searching for me." "Why would I give up on my best friend in the whole world?" said Aoife. "I could never, ever, do that to my best friend." "Aoife! I'm glad you found me; that you didn't give up. You are a true friend." I had introduced Aoife to our secret greeting code – the one I had started with Brownie. With that, we rubbed our noses together and raised our right paws to honor and continue to pledge our loyalty to each other. "What about Brownie?" I asked Aoife. "Have you seen him or heard from him?" "No!" she said. "I searched for him like I searched for you but I couldn't find him. He must have been taken away by Farmer Jim in his trailer." "Oh! That's not possible. That could never happen," I replied. "Knowing Brownie, he wouldn't have wanted to go with Farmer Jim. Of course, he wanted to be with his friends forever. Like the two of us, he wanted us all to grow up, eat lots of grass, get fat, get old together, and still enjoy with each other." "I believe you," said Aoife. "But where else would he have gone? He just wouldn't disappear without telling us. "I suggested to Aoife that the two of us should stay together and search for Brownie. We did that for days.

No luck! We even asked the other lambs and sheep if they had seen him. No one had.Sadly, we had to admit that Brownie was kidnapped along with the other lambs by Farmer Jim. We know that he didn't want to go with Farmer Jim but, it seems, he had no other choice.

That night, the two of us slept together.
We hugged each other and cried because we missed Brownie.
He was part of the two of us. We were family. He was part of our trinity of love. We looked up at the starry sky with all its little lights giving light to a dark world. Even the moon was a new moon, letting us know the best is yet to come. I turned to Aoife, as a tear trickled down her pretty face. I hugged her and said, "Maybe, Brownie is looking down on us from up there! Maybe, he wants to tell us that although he is no longer physically present with us, he is with us in spirit. Maybe, he wants us to continue making friends, to continue breaking down barriers, to stop judging by outward appearances, and, instead, see the beauty within. We are all gifts to each other but that gift can be seen only through the heart."

"I have a feeling that Brownie wants us to continue, too," suggested Aoife. "We've got work to do. Let's do it. Let's get some rest now. Tomorrow is a new day."As she said this, I thought, All of our lives will never be the same again. We are changed forever.

Freckles and Dara.....Reflection questions – Children

(Parents may use the following reflections or similar ones to generate a discussion with their child/children)

1. At school or at play, do children call each other "Names?" Names like "smart," "stupid," "ugly," "bully," "Jerk," etc.? What names have you heard being used? How do you think that makes the person being called that name feels?

2. Have you ever being called "Names?" When did it happen? How did you react? How did it make you feel?

3. Why do you think children call each other "names?" Often these "Names" are not very nice. The person who calls another child a "name", what are they trying to do? to prove? Do they succeed?

4. Are their child/children in your school and/or neighbourhood that don't have any friends? Why do you think that is so? Are they scared? Have they been hurt by a friend in the past? Why do you think?

5. Do you know what a "bully" is? Are there any in your school/neighbourhood? Why do they act that way? What are they trying to achieve? Does the bully have friends that always backs him/her up? Why do you think it is important that a bully has to have such people to back them up?

6. Have you ever being bullied in school or in the neighbourhood? Would you like to share what happened, how you reacted, and what you did about it. Did you walk away? Fight back? Ignore him/her? Plan ways to get them back?

7. Freckles and Dara tried to make friends with everyone. Was this a good idea? Was it worth it? Were they just naive? What were they really trying to do?

8. Is it easier for children to made friends with other children rather than adults trying to make friends with other adults? If that is so, what do you think is the reasons? Are? Is it worth it? Why are you children more trusting but adults seem to be more suspicious or jealous of other adults?

9. Have you been hurt by your friends? Have they ever said mean things about you behind your back? If so, how did that make your feel? What did you learn from finding it out?

10. What do you think the story of Freckles and Dara is trying to teach us? Does it make sense? What would the world be like if we followed the example of Freckles and Dara? What kind of things can you do to help spread Freckles and Dara's message?

Freckles and Dara .....Reflection questions – Adults

(Adults may use the following reflections or similar ones to generate a discussion with their peers)

1. As adults, we are very good at putting "labels" on other adults; labels like "know-it-all," "ignorant," "has to be always right," "gossiper," "never shuts up, " etc. Why are "labels" so important in an adult world? How do we use them? Why? What do they achieve?

2. By putting a "label" on another person, do we feel better knowing where we stand with that person? How to relate better to that person?

3. Do "labels" feel less threatened by other adults? If so, why? Do "labels" give us more security or make us more insecure around such persons?

4. In your work environment, what are some of the posturing and/or politicking that fellow workers engage in? What are they trying to accomplish? Is it healthy or toxic?

5. Society often talks about "profiling" people. Why? How does it happen? What does it accomplish?

6. Have you as a child being on the giving or receiving end of profiling? Why? How did it happen> How did it shape your outlook on life as an adult?

7. Have you ever felt that you didn't fit in? That you were a loner? That people didn't understand you?

8. Daily, we hear such words as "acceptance," "judgment," "first impressions," "prejudice," "racist," "bigoted," etc. Do we feel uncomfortable with the use of such words? Are they too emotive sometimes? Do they threaten us or make us re-evaluate our outlook and perceptions of people and situations in general? Why so?

9. Society has different ways of measuring personal success or failure. What are the different ways? Are they honest? Legitimate? Most efficient? How should a person's success or failure be measured?

10. Freckles and Dara are naïve? Unrealistic? To be commended? They cannot change people? Worth a try? What would the world be like if we followed Dara fable is this.........

# About the Author

Michael Tracey served as a Catholic priest in Mississippi, U.S.A., from 1972 until his retirement in 2013. He served in various parish and diocesan ministries including Director of Youth Ministry, Director of RENEW, and Director of Campus Ministry. He continues as a regular columnist for a Mississippi newspaper since 1976. He is the author of Woman of the Cloth, Walking Shoes, May the Wind…, She Was No Lady, The Crooked Christmas Tree, A Journey with Boreen, and his latest, Freckles and Dara. He was honored as the 'Mayo Person of the Year' in 2008 by the Boston Mayo Association for his rebuilding efforts of his community in Mississippi following the devastation of Hurricane Katrina in August 2005. His claim to fame is that he was the proud recipient of a hole-in-one in golf. In his retirement, he enjoys writing, photography, videography, and organic gardening, in Ireland, where he resides.

* 9 7 8 1 8 3 9 3 4 8 6 5 5 *